THE UPSIDE-DOWN CAT

THE UPSIDE-
DOWN CAT

by Elizabeth Parsons

illustrated by Ronald Himler

A Margaret K. McElderry Book

Atheneum 1981 *New York*

Library of Congress Cataloging in Publication Data

Parsons, Elizabeth.
  The upside-down cat.
  "A Margaret K. McElderry book."
  SUMMARY: A young boy learns a difficult but important
lesson about life when he discovers his cat, missing
since the previous summer, living happily with an old
fisherman.
  [1. Cats — Fiction] I. Himler, Ronald.
II. Title.
PZ7.P2526Up   [Fic]   80-13507
ISBN 0-689-50187-0

Text copyright © 1981 by Elizabeth Parsons
Illustrations copyright © 1981 by Ronald Himler
All rights reserved
Published simultaneously in Canada by McClelland & Stewart, Ltd.
Composed by American–Stratford Graphic Services, Inc.,
Brattleboro, Vermont
Printed by Holliday Lithograph Corporation,
West Hanover, Massachusetts
Designed by Maria Epes
Bound by A. Horowitz & Sons/Bookbinders,
Fairfield, New Jersey
First Edition

For Max

I

There was a cat, once, called Lily Black. That was her name because she was marked in black and white — as white as a lily and as black as coal. She was a handsome little cat, with her white bib and her four white paws like short socks. Her face was comical, with a dab of white right on her nose and whiskers that curled so much they almost met in front. It was a round face, and her enormous green eyes were as round as dimes and looked you right in the eye in a way that was disconcerting in a cat. She had the prettiest ears in the world, set just right on her head, with each furry tip turned back a bit, like the tip of a leaf. She was tidy and pleased with herself in general — and why shouldn't she be, as nobody had ever said a harsh word to her or had to punish her. She liked people, for the most part; dogs and other cats she ignored whenever she could.

When this story begins, she lived in a very small brick house hidden away at the end of an alley in the middle of New York City — such a tiny house that it had only three rooms, one on each of its floors, plus an attic. A long time ago it had been a farmhouse, and it still smelled like one — of cooking and animals and sooty chimney flues and layers of old wallpapers. There was a fireplace in each room, and that's all the heat there was, even now. It was a cozy house to find there in a great city, tucked away secretly, with high buildings all around. When you were in it you could almost imagine you were far away in the country, with fields outside the kitchen door and cows coming up the alley (which had once been a lane) to be milked in a barn that had been torn down long ago to make room for apartment houses. Lily Black could race up and down the steep stairs and skid all over the slippery floors and climb the two locust trees that had managed to keep growing in the cement courtyard, and it all suited her very well. She had come there as a tiny kitten. The butcher around the corner, one day when he was delivering some meat to the little house, had pulled her out of the pocket of his white coat and handed her to Joe, along with the meat. "I got too many — take her," said the butcher, and turned away in a hurry.

There were four of them in the household: Pa, Mother, Joe — who had just turned seven — and Lily Black. Joe looked a little like some shy, wild animal — it would be hard to say which one — with hair the color of a red squirrel's coat and very light brown eyes that didn't miss much. He was almost as quick and neat as Lily herself, and he wasn't at all talkative. Mostly he kept his thoughts to himself, except for whispering to Lily when they were in bed at night, and he told her everything that had happened or had been on his mind all day.

Early in her life, Lily Black had developed a very odd habit. An iron register had been set into the kitchen ceiling, to let the heat go up to the room above in cold weather, and ever since she had been big enough to climb the stairs, Lily had spent a lot of time lying on this register, soaking up the warmth that came wafting up, smelling of pot roast or pie or popovers or whatever Mother was cooking. For quite a while Pa objected to this.

"Get her off there!" he would order Joe. "She's taking up all the

4

heat. Get her off!" But he gave up after a while; he knew a lost cause when he saw one. What was *really* odd was that Lily Black wasn't sleeping much of the time she was lying there, as an ordinary cat would. She would lie on her back with her white paws flopping on her white shirtfront and her head turned to one side or the other, looking at the life going on in the kitchen below — upside down. She would lie there for hours at a time, hot as a biscuit.

So that's how she came to be referred to as the "Upside-Down Cat." People coming to the house would look up to see if she were there, watching them from that strange position with her green eyes half-closed. If she wasn't lying there they always asked, "Where's the Upside-Down Cat?"

Probably she did take up a good deal of valuable heat, but nobody minded except Pa.

2

Every year, when summer came, they packed up the car and went off to Maine, where they had a house just as small as the city one, but it seemed much bigger because it was all on one level and was full of sunshine all day long. There were huge windows on three sides looking out over a landlocked loop of the sea that was called "The Basin." From there they couldn't see a single house, or hear any cars — no sounds but the birds and the wind in the spruce trees and sometimes the engine of a lobsterman's boat chugging along slowly on The Basin and, on foggy days and nights, the calls of ships' whistles far away. Out beyond and below, to the south, lay the open Atlantic and a lot of wooded islands edged with pale gray rocks. There were two lighthouses whose flashes Joe liked to count at night. To the east was Green's Island (five flashes), and Barton's Ledge (two longs and a short) to the south. He could see them both from his bed when Lily, worn out from her day's hunting, slept soundly at his feet.

So Lily Black had two lives. She had the good, protected city life in the winter, and every summer it was exchanged for a free country life.

This particular summer, when Joe was ten and Lily Black was three, started off just as usual. One June day they drove up to the house above The Basin and it was all exactly as they had left it last fall. The late-afternoon wind was blowing hard up the rocky face of the hill, and big, golden-headed thunderclouds were piling up in the west. They were all so happy to be back that they almost cried — all except Lily, who gave a quick look around and a few sniffs, knew where she was, and disappeared over the moss and the bristly grass and into the woods, her round eyes bigger than ever.

Although of course she didn't know it, her upside-down life stopped then, for a long time to come.

3

The summer passed quickly and happily for everyone. Joe had an old punt he was allowed to row anywhere in, as long as he didn't go outside The Basin. Every morning Pa went off to his "study," as he rather grandly called a little old building somewhat away from the house. He was writing a book. Mother planted and tended the rows of lettuces and peas and herbs, with zinnias and poppies and other bright flowers here and there, and wrote long letters to faraway friends. They went swimming in the warm Basin and they had picnics and they went clamming, and so the days passed, much too fast.

As for Lily Black, she spent her time roaming far and wide through the woods and along the shore. She covered a lot of ground, and she got rather thin, and often she stayed away for the night, or for a day or two. Nobody worried about her absences, as they knew she knew where she was.

"She uses us as though we were a first-class hotel," Pa would say now and then, rather testily. "Just drops in when she wants a good meal and a soft bed." The others had sense enough not to say anything to that: they knew Pa was crazy about Lily, whatever he might pretend. (They also knew she often dropped in at his study to take a nap on his camp cot, and he had an idea he worked better when she was there.)

So the days went by, and just before Labor Day Lily Black's life suffered a tremendous change.

The weather was cool and sunny, and there was a huge moon for what seemed like a whole week while it waxed and waned in the clear sky, and the stars were as bright as stars are far out at sea, and back in the woods the owls hooted softly all night. Lily was restless, with the enormous moon, and she was wandering farther and farther away.

Then one day around sunrise, she found she didn't know where she was — she who thought she knew every inch of the countryside for miles around. Somewhere or other on the far shore of The Basin she

had crossed a tarred road and gotten into perfectly strange territory. She wanted to go home, for she had already been away two days and three nights — but where *was* home?

She wandered this way and that, slowly, sitting down every so often to try to figure out where she was. She drank out of little brooks and she ate whatever she came across and she slept (not soundly) under blueberry bushes or in beds of fern. Lost! Never in her life had anything so scary happened to her. Poor Lily gave small, forlorn mews as she walked along, sounding like a very young kitten and not the grown-up cat that she was. If anyone had come along just then and heard her, she would have been gathered up into kind arms, and her sad mewing would have turned to a loud purring. But there was no one to hear her. Lily Black was completely lost.

Night came, and the moon rose — late, now — over the black, pointed spruces, and in the black shadows Lily's black markings were invisible as she went secretly along. Once she ran across a dog's trail, so she became even more wary after sniffing this unwelcome smell in the resinous woods. All around her was salt water; whichever way she went she always came to it. The fact was, she had gone out onto a point of land between The Basin and the sea — gone a long way, miles and miles from home. She wandered aimlessly along, and from then on she led the life of a gypsy cat, without any friends or any shelter, all on her own as the autumn came in. At first she was often homesick and would begin her small mewing, but then stop it in case some other animal heard her. She was never very hungry as there was plenty to eat, but she had to work to get it.

4

Lily's family had begun to worry about her. "She's never been gone for so long," they kept saying to each other. "What could have happened to her?" They had terrible thoughts about raccoons and wild tomcats and hound dogs and mink traps and all kinds of perilous things, and twice Joe walked all the way around The Basin (which involved wading across the entrance at low tide), calling over and over, "Lily! Lily Black! Come-come-come! Supper-supper-supper! Come, Lily!" But, as we know, Lily Black was far away and couldn't possibly have heard him, even if the wind was right. If she *had* heard him, you can bet she would have come racing through the woods. She would have picked up his trail and followed it at last to the house where everyone would pet her and tell her how wonderful she was, how beautiful and clever, and chide her for being gone so long and worrying them so much. She would eat a good supper and have a long, solid sleep beside Joe, on his red bedspread.

Mother could hear Joe, though — hear his anxious voice growing fainter and fainter as he walked farther and farther away, scrambling over dead trees and along the rocks at the edge of the water, and then growing louder and sadder and slower as he came nearer again. When he was home, she hugged him tight, and he hugged her and went into his room and shut the door.

11

Now Joe was finding out what a house was like without a cat in it. He worried most of the day about Lily and at night he worried even more, as people do when they're lonesome. Sometimes he cried in bed by himself. Because, after all, Joe and Mother and Pa had to go back to the city right after Labor Day. They *had* to go, because of Joe's school and Pa's work. Joe thought he and Mother should stay behind and wait for Lily, who would surely come home when the cold weather set in, and let Pa go on ahead. He himself, he said, could perfectly well start school right there. He could walk out to the town road and catch the school bus.

"Joe, dear, we just can't," his mother said. "You know that doesn't make sense. Lily may *never* come back — you know that." She wouldn't say what she really felt, which was that Lily Black was dead.

They had put a notice in the post office and on the movie screen (LOST! from The Basin, small black and white cat, answers to name of Lily Black. REWARD!"), but nobody answerd. They had asked everyone they met for miles around, but no one had even seen her.

"Guess she got caught in a trap, or somebody stole her," said one old woman they asked, and that upset them, as it was just the kind of thing they had themselves been imagining but had not been able to mention.

"Mean old thing," said Joe, and Pa answered, "Yes, she always was."

So finally they packed the car and made the last trip into town to say goodbye to their friends and pay their bills, and they cleaned out the icebox and pulled down the shades and took a last look at the sky and the gulls and the blue sea and the dark islands, and then they drove away, feeling that they had abandoned a member of the family to a terrible fate. They would have felt better if they had known for sure that she was dead, and not suffering, dying slowly in a mink trap or being driven crazy by cruel children who had stolen her, exactly as the old woman had suggested.

Anyway, they left. It couldn't be helped.

5

It was getting cold at night now, and Lily began to grow a warm coat; this year it grew in earlier and thicker than usual in the cool country autumn. She recovered her good spirits, and as a matter of fact she was quite happy, but she never slept very soundly for she was afraid of whatever big animals there might be in the woods.

The weeks went by, and the harvest moon came and went, and so did the hunter's moon, and the ground froze, and then came the first light snow. Lily Black wasn't used to snow in the country; she picked her way along uncomfortably, her paws sinking in and her tail held carefully up.

One sunny afternoon, when the snow had mostly melted, she was hunting along the shore in a new direction when she came out in a small clearing, and there, close by, almost at high-water mark, was a little building, somebody's fish house, with a spindly wharf running out into a narrow, deep cove. What good smells she smelled there! Fish and woodsmoke and a hot iron stove and a person — just one person, she knew. Smoke wavered up out of the stovepipe in the roof, as though

the fire inside was almost out. The door of the house was shut tight,
and the one window, too. Nobody was there *then*, but somebody had
been there not long before. Lily looked things over for a while, sitting
at the edge of the woods; then she went very carefully around sniffing
at everything. By the door there was a bent old wicker armchair with a
sagging seat. Then she crawled in under the house and — O joy! — there
was an old cushion stuffed in under the floor. *It* smelled of kitchens and
workpants, and the stuffing was coming out here and there. Lily sat
down on it and washed up, feeling safe and almost at home, and then
she went to sleep — a real sleep for the first time in weeks. The cushion
was so soft that she sank deep into it as she slept, curled up into a tight,
warm ball.

14

6

All this was so nice that Lily Black decided to stay there. Why not, indeed? She had a warm, dry bed, and nobody was around, so she settled in.

She had been there for three days, very content with things, when the owner of the fish house came along, catching her by surprise. One sunny day when she was on her way back along the path from the woods, she realized that someone was at the house. Smoke was going up out of the stovepipe at a great rate, and the door was open and a beautiful smell of lobster stew drifted out to her. That smell made her give her sad little mew. She couldn't help it: it came out of her throat before she could stop it. Then she sat down, half-hidden by a low juniper branch, to watch.

Pretty soon a very tall and heavy old man came to the door and dumped a panful of water out on the frozen ground. He took a look at the sky and went back in and shut the door, but not before the smell of the stew had made Lily Black quite bold. She went nearer and nearer to the house, moving from bush to bush. In a little while the old man came out again, and this time he left, slamming the door and thumping off down the wharf that shook under him and rowing away in his yellow skiff. He hadn't bothered to put out the fire in the stove, though, and Lily liked that smell of smoke that she knew so well. She went up to the house and sat in the chair awhile; she dozed there, with her eyes closed to slits in the low sunlight, wondering about this and that.

Lily Black had the place to herself for a few days, but one morning under the house she was waked up by the sound of someone walking up the wharf and then thudding over the floor just above her head, and there was a great banging of stove lids and the rumble of somebody talking to himself. There was the crackle of kindling wood lighting up, and some heavy knocks as two big rubber boots were kicked off. Lily lay very still, taking no chances, but she was terribly curious.

Pretty soon there came down through the chinks in the floor the alluring smell of fish chowder heating up. It was too much for Lily Black, who, truth to tell, was getting a little tired of her wildwood diet. Very cautiously she got up, stretched, and very slowly crept out and peeked in at the side of the door that was kept partway open to let in some fresh air. There she saw her new companion, in heavy pants and a green and black checked shirt, standing in his stocking feet beside the stove, stirring something in a saucepan. He looked very peaceable, mumbling comfortably to himself and stirring away. Lily forgot to be careful, she was so taken by all this, and she walked up to the middle of the threshold and sat down. But it was all right. The old man saw her sitting there with a beseeching air, and instead of shouting and throwing a boot at her, as somebody else might have done at a stray cat, he looked at her kindly, with his big spoon in the air. Then he said, "Mornin', Miss Kitty. Come in and have somethin' to eat."

Kitty! Come!

Lily had known about ten words, once, and now she recognized two

16

of them. But more than that, she recognized something in the old man's voice, something gentle and loving, that was very familiar to her. She walked delicately into the room, and it was as though her gypsy months faded away from her right then — gone! She sat down in front of her new friend as though she had known him forever and looked up into his face that badly needed shaving and let out a loud but very polite *miaow*, a regular cat *miaow*, not the pitiful mewing of her first lonely days.

"Hungry, are ye?" he said to her. "And lost too, I bet. You ain't been around *here* before, I know." He ladled some chowder out into a small bowl and blew on it to cool it off and put it down in front of her, and she bent her head and ate. Oh, how good it was! She ate the whole bowlful, of course, and gave him a very grateful look and sat back and washed herself all around her face and her front paws.

"Pretty Miss Kitty," said the old man admiringly, watching this procedure. He had filled a bowl for himself and was sitting at the round table, eating. He gave them each some more and they ate that up and Lily washed once again. The old man hitched his chair up nearer the stove and lit his pipe and said to her, "Yes, you're a real pretty little cat, and smart too, I can tell. Somebody at home misses you, I dare say." As he never went to the post office or the movies he hadn't seen the notices that Lily's family had put up last fall.

As for Lily, she jumped up onto his lap and began to purr furiously, as though to make up for lost time, and licked his hard, salty old hand as well. She was beside herself with happiness. As for the old man, he was tickled to death with her and stroked her and told her how pretty she was and how glad he was to have her there, and they were well pleased with each other. Then the old man set his pipe down in a saucer on the table and fell sound asleep; seeing this, Lily settled herself on his lap and slept too, while the wood snapped softly in the stove and the oblong piece of sunlight on the floor inside the open door moved from left to right and got narrower and narrower and finally disappeared entirely while the two new friends were lost to the world.

7

They woke up after an hour or so, and Lily Black went over to the doorway and sat down, perfectly at home. The old man pulled on his boots and went out to work on the lobster traps he was building. He didn't set out very many nowadays, though he had once been a famous fisherman — just a couple of dozen now, mostly to give himself something to do and as an excuse to get away from home and be by himself. So he pounded away that cold afternoon and Lily sat near him and he talked to her now and then, as though she was a person.

"Well, Kitty," he said at one point, "I'd like to take you home with me, but I can't. I love cats myself, but I can't have one 'cause my wife she just hates 'em. Scairt to death of 'em, so I ain't had a cat at all since I been married. But I tell you what we'll do. I come up here two or three times a week anyway, and I'll bring you some food every time, and if you stick around here that'll take care o' you in good shape. You're nice and snug here under the building, and you'll be all right. How's that?" He was very pleased himself with this arrangement, as he really did love cats and he hadn't had one since he was growing up on his father's farm — and now one had come to him right out of the blue.

"Yes, we'll be company for each other," he told her. "You just stay around." He began to laugh then, as Lily had got hold of a short piece of pot warp and was rushing around in circles with it dangling out of her mouth — then letting it go and pouncing on it, pretending it was a grass snake.

The sun was getting low by this time and the old man had to stop work and put his tools away and shut up the house. He picked Lily up and petted her, and she clung onto his thick shirt with her claws. He

carried her out on his shoulder to the end of the wharf and there he had to pull her off and put her down, though he didn't want to. He untied his skiff and went down the ladder until his face was level with hers, and they stared at each other, blue eyes and green eyes.

"Take care o' yourself, Miss Kitty," he said, scratching her gently under the chin. "I'll see you Sunday." There was a lump in his throat as he said that, for some reason, something he hadn't known for a long time. Lily, in return, gave his hand three little nudges, just as she used to give Joe's.

Poor Lily Black, sitting on the end of the wharf, watching her friend row away and leave her! She looked after him until he had disappeared around a point of land, and then she walked slowly back to shore, her tail hanging down.

But by the door she found a bowl of chowder that had been set out for her supper.

Sunday came, a gloomy day with snow in the air, and sure enough when Lily was not far away from the house, doing a little hunting, she heard the creaking of rowlocks. She went straight to the edge of the clearing and sat down to see what would happen next. It was her friend, as she knew right away when he got to the door, and she trotted up, miaowing very energetically and, I fear, demandingly.

"Why, there you are!" said the old man, bending down to stroke her and to pull her tail gently. (She loved that.) "So you're still here, I'm glad to say. Come right in. I brought you somethin' good for your dinner. Hamburg!"

They went indoors, and it was exactly like the time before. The fire was started and the room got so hot the door had to be left open a little, and the two of them ate all the hamburg they wanted — a lot — and then they had a good nap. Sometimes the old man snored and twitched a little in his sleep, and Lily herself wheezed and purred softly on his lap.

That day the old man didn't work outdoors — he felt kind of lazy and he stayed inside, cleaning up some tools and filing a saw, humming to himself, and Lily Black sat in his rocking chair by the table, perfectly happy. When he had finished his chores, he took a harmonica off a shelf and blew into it, running up and down its length a few times, trying it out.

"It's a long time since I played this," he said to Lily. "But now I got an audience, I might as well practice up." First he played slowly and sadly, songs from his boyhood, and then he got more lively and played reels and jigs that he had danced to when he was young and quite a hand with the girls, keeping time with one stocking foot and swinging his white head smartly to and fro. Lily liked this commotion a lot; perhaps she remembered the noise and the fun when she lay on the register and looked down at people cavorting around in the kitchen of the little city house a year ago.

But then, of course, the old man had to go home to the wife who was scared of cats. He put the harmonica away on the shelf, hauled his boots on, and he and Lily Black went out into the cold air. He picked her up

and carried her on his shoulder out to the end of the wharf, and there he set her down, just as before, and she watched him row away, only this time their parting wasn't sad.

"See you on Tuesday!" he called back to her in his big voice. "You be a good girl and hang around!" She trotted briskly ashore, and again she found a bowl of food by the doorstep.

That's the way life went along, all through the winter. Christmas came, and the old man brought Lily some turkey he'd sneaked from his daughter-in-law's family dinner. New Year's Day came and went, and there was a lot of snow and cold, windy weather after that. The ice was thick in the cove, a dirty yellow color, and it built up around the old man's wharf so he couldn't land there but had to walk up from further along the shore where the ice was thin. Bluejays screamed in the trees and the red squirrels scattered spruce cones all over the place. After every snowstorm the heavy snow would slide off the spruce boughs and thump softly down here and there through the woods. There were little tracks all around, but Lily Black found that hunting was hard work, as she sank far down into the snow, and everything she liked best to eat seemed to be underground most of the time. It was a good thing for her that the old man came so often and looked after her so well, otherwise she might have come close to starving to death.

They were a happy pair, these two. Now and then the old man would spend the night at the fish house, and that was a real treat for Lily. He had some quilts on the bunk in the corner, and there he slept with Lily rolled up beside him as round as a sleeping woolly bear caterpillar, warm and safe. Truth to tell, he got so fond of her that he came more often than he usually did in the winter, to make sure she was all right. His wife didn't understand why he stayed away from home so much, and of course he didn't tell her. He said he'd decided to set out more traps this spring than last year and that he had to shingle the roof of the little building, and that was all quite true though it was only part of the story. Lily was his own secret, for the time being anyway.

The old man talked a lot to Lily and she would sit watching his face and purring. Sometimes she talked back, little squawks strung together almost like a sentence with a miaowlike squeak added here and there for emphasis. He never did think of just the right name for her; he called her Miss Kitty most of the time. She didn't like it when he went away and left her alone, but now she knew he'd be back. She stayed pretty close to home while he was gone and grew fat again.

As for the old man, when he came rowing in he would look first for a good place on the ice to pull his boat up and then for his cat. If she wasn't around he would call her and she would come running, delighted to see him as well as being anxious for a good meal.

The old man tore one page after another off the hardware store calendar that hung by the bunk as the winter passed and spring came. The ice went out. The snow melted and so did the ground. The grass around the house now had green blades that Lily Black ate greedily, and one very warm day a patch of gravel was so dry that she lay down on it and had a good scratch, to and fro, to and fro on her back in the hot, gritty dirt. Once she stopped all of a sudden and lay absolutely still, on her back, with her front paws dangling and her head turned back and to one side, just as she had lain so much of the time when she was the Upside-Down Cat. She lay that way for so long that the old man, who was sitting in his outdoor chair to rest awhile, noticed her and said, "Why are you lyin' like that, Miss Kitty? Not sick, are ye?" At that she sprang up and went tearing off, dashing around in big circles with her ears laid back and her tail straight up in the air, making the old man laugh.

9

Spring!

Lily Black began to shed and had to be combed a lot.

One morning not long after April Fool's Day, the old man decided to start setting out his traps, so he brought his lobster boat — the *Lettie V.* — in to his wharf at high water and unloaded a tub of bait. He baited up twelve traps, stuffing the fish into the little mesh bags that his wife knitted for him out of twine when she didn't have anything else to do or was feeling nervous. First, however, he fed Lily, who was on hand and curious about his doings. She ate, and then she poked her head into the bait tub and drew back in a hurry. When the old man began to carry his traps to the boat and load them on board, she wandered around in an uncertain way, staying near him. When he'd got all the traps loaded, the old man started the engine with a roar, and Lily fled under the house and from there she peeked out and watched him back the *Lettie V.* away and head out past the point. This time he hadn't said goodbye to her.

He was back in the afternoon, rowing in from his mooring, and sat down in his chair by the door to have a smoke and a rest, and Lily lay on the grass near him, squinting in the low, hot sunshine. Out beyond the shelter of the cove, whitecaps and dark blue seas raced away fast, and the wind made a steady humming in the tops of the trees. Birds were coming

26

north now, and they were singing in the woods and calling along the shore. It was a fine day, all in all, with the winter gone and the two friends content together.

Lily Black, however, was in for some surprises.

10

The old man ended by setting out thirty-two traps in all — just enough to give himself something to do, as he said to his fishermen friends. He came, as usual, to attend to things around the place and to look after his little cat.

One day when he was leaving to go home and Lily Black was out on the end of the wharf bidding him goodbye, he said to her, "Come on now, Miss Catlubber, come for a row with me!" And he swooped her up and shoved the skiff out from the wharf before she had a chance to leap ashore, and there she was in a wobbling boat out on the water, terrified! She huddled between his feet as he picked up his oars and rowed along slowly. The boat rocked a little, and the small motion frightened Lily half to death. What was happening, and why should her kind friend be doing this to her? The old man talked to her and now and then stopped rowing to pet her, and pretty soon she realized there was nothing so terrible going on and she sat up, putting her front paws in a gingerly way on the gunwale and looking first down at the water and then up at the old man, balancing herself neatly and trying to figure out this predicament.

"Ah-ha," he said to her. "You see it's not so bad, is it, old girl? Maybe you'd like to be a sailor's cat and come fishin' with me." Then he rowed her back to the wharf, kissed her on top of the head, and set her out safe and sound. As he rowed off he thought she stared after him with a very interested expression.

"We'll go again," he called back to her. "That's a promise!"

It was a promise that he kept, and he and Lily Black became a subject of conversation among the other fishermen and, in time, a legend. He gave up his secret, but it was worth it.

"Remember that little black cat old Henry used to take to haul with him?" people would say for years to come, every so often. "Quite a sight, that was."

Because Lily did indeed prove to be a sailor's cat. First the old man took her for a row every day he was there, just for fun, and he'd chuckle to himself to see her getting used to being on the water, which is not a very natural place for a cat to be. She now sat up very straight and perky on the stern thwart, looking all around with great curiosity.

In fact, he was so much amused by her behavior that one day he put her on board the *Lettie V.* to see what she made of that, while he did some work on the engine. At first, she was offended by the smell of fish, for though the old man was very neat, you can't keep a lobster boat from smelling of the things it's used for. Lily padded around in a finicky way, trying to walk where the smell was least. She went into the cuddy and came out again in no time, and finally she settled down on the afterdeck where it was fresh and pleasant. When it was suppertime they both went ashore again.

That was the beginning of the Upside-Down Cat's seafaring life.

She went out in the boat only in good weather. When it rained or blew hard she stayed on her cushion under the house and waited for the old man to come in. Not for her the cold wind coming all the way from Portugal or Greenland, the rain slanting off along the tops of the gray seas and the *Lettie V.* rolling and pitching, no *sir*. But on fine days, there she was, sitting up on deck as they moved slowly around the shore and once a week went up into The Basin where the old man had also set out a few traps this year. The other fishermen as they passed would wave to him and shout, "My Godfrey Mighty, Henry — what's that creature you got there?" Or, "Got a new hand, I see!"

When they got back to the harbor and were sitting around the fishermen's store somebody might say, "You know, Henry's got a cat that goes out to haul with him?"

"No!" some newcomer would exclaim, and somebody else would say, "Well, he's always been kind of odd, Henry has. Hope his old woman don't find out." Because everybody knew about the cat phobia that Henry's wife had; it had been local gossip for years, in a joking way. And she never did find out. The old man had given his secret away to his friends, but it was safe with them.

At the fish house, about now, the old man tore another page off his calendar and "JUNE" stood out in large black letters edged with scarlet at the top of the new page.

As the month went on, there didn't seem to be much nighttime. By half-past three it was dawn and the birds were singing, and in the evening it didn't get dark until nearly ten o'clock. There was a huge moon, too, bright enough to read by. Lily Black roamed all night long, creeping through the new ferns and over the thick mosses, but taking good care not to get too far from home. That was one lesson she had learned only too well to forget ever again for the rest of her life.

One morning, when she had gone out with the old man in the *Lettie V.* to haul the few traps he had set in The Basin, guess what happened.

II

Joe and his family had come back the week before. It was a real homecoming for them, seeing everything again, looking up their old friends and opening the house and sweeping up the thousands of dead flies and letting the warm wind blow through the rooms. They bought paint and new flashlight batteries and seeds, and they planted the vegetable garden and the little flowerbed.

One thing they often mentioned as they went about these familiar chores: they still had the idea that perhaps Lily Black was alive and that she'd know they were there now, and when she got good and ready she'd come back.

"If she's anywhere around, I *know* she'll know we're back," Joe told himself every day, very determined.

He painted his punt — a good bright orange outside and blue-green inside — and launched her, and the first day he took her out he rowed so far he got terrible blisters on the insides of his thumbs. He went for a row every day, happy to be out on the water again. The wonderful thing was to come back year after year and find things just as he remembered them — the colors and the smells and the big landscape, and his old clothes and books and treasures right where he'd left them. The smells were the best, after the city — the woods and the sea and the clam flats, and the creosote on the shingles of your house on a hot sunny day. Then there was the rainspout splashing into the rain barrel outside your window when you were going to sleep on a stormy night. It had been best when Lily Black had been curled up beside him, dry and warm and safe, just as he was.

Only this year there was no little cat. But Joe refused to give up hoping.

Generally, in the morning, if the tide was right and The Basin was

32

brimming with the water that rushed in from the sea through the narrow entrance, he would make the round of his favorite places. He would maneuver through tiny passages where he had to pole his way along with an oar, or he would go ashore on some bare little island and lie for a while in the prickly grass. There was one with a beach of real sand, about as big as his bedroom on the hill, between two high rocks, and he would have a swim there. He had made his parents a promise about swimming. "You can go in alone," Pa told him, "just as long as you can put one toe on the bottom — no deeper," and he was very good about sticking to that rule.

One morning, when he was rowing along, he noticed a small lobster boat he hadn't seen in The Basin before, going from buoy to buoy in

a leisurely way, and pretty soon their paths began to cross, and when they were quite close the bigger boat stopped while its owner bent over and caught hold of the trap he had just hauled up. Joe was admiring the boat's pretty lines and fresh gray paint when he saw something so peculiar, so ridiculous, that he stopped rowing to have a good look. What he was seeing was a little black and white cat, sitting bolt upright on the stern deck.

"Lily!" he shouted, without even thinking. "Lily! Lily Black!"

The little cat stood up at that, staring right at him, and Joe rowed up alongside, hardly able to believe his eyes, and yet — and yet! *Could* it be Lily? Could it possibly be, sitting there on a strange boat, of all places? The old fisherman, whose back had been turned, but who had heard Joe call out, now heard him say, "That *is* you, Lily! I know that's you! I knew you'd turn up — I knew it!" and he looked around at the boy whose red head was not much above the deck of the *Lettie V.*

Joe was so excited that he forgot everything. All he wanted to do was grab up his cat and row away as fast as he could.

"That's my cat!" he said rudely, in his excitement, to the old man. "We lost her last summer, just when we were leaving. I mean, she disappeared when we were leaving. I know that's her!"

The old man took his time about all this. "Good mornin'," he said, as though nothing peculiar was going on. "I've seen you before. Live up on the hill, summers, don't ye?"

"Yes, we do," said Joe, and the old man's calmness made him remember his own manners, and he set his oars down along the thwarts, very businesslike, and stood up, holding on with one hand to the *Lettie V.*'s rail and reaching out the other one to Lily Black. *Then* Lily came up to him, purring, and licked his hand and nudged it hard with her head, waving her tail to and fro.

"Well, I guess she knows you, all right," said the old man, looking at the two of them wonderingly. "She came way over to my place, on the Point." He jerked his head in the direction of his fish house. "She turned up there early last winter and I took her in. She's a real nice little cat, and I'm glad you got her back."

But he wasn't a hundred percent glad. He had never really expected to lose her, certainly not this way. He was caught by surprise and it was a hard thing to bear — but he *was* going to lose her, right there and then, without any warning at all.

Joe was petting Lily Black, and she was remembering — what? Who knows, but *something*, something from a long time back.

Then the old man said, and his voice sounded not at all right to himself, "There, you take her now. Take her home. Go along with you, Miss Kitty, and be a good girl and don't you go strayin' off again." And in one second he had caught her up and handed her to Joe and pushed the punt away out of reach with a great shove. In fact, Joe nearly fell overboard with Lily in his arms, and he sat down quickly.

Lily Black hopped up where she could see everything and suddenly realized that she was being parted from her good old friend, and she looked from one human face to the other in some puzzled cat distress, while the distance between the boats slowly grew wider and wider. She seemed so troubled that for a minute Joe thought she would jump overboard and swim back to the *Lettie V.*, but luckily she didn't.

"So long," the old man said, and Joe answered, "So long." Later he remembered he hadn't even said thank you.

The old man started up his engine and went off to his next trap. "Better so," he told himself. "She ought to be where she belongs, where she'll be taken care of properly, 'cause one o' these days I may not be around to look after her at all. But I'll miss her, yes I will."

He decided not to bother to haul any more that day, but to go on home. He didn't even stop at the fish house: he didn't feel like seeing the empty dishes on the floor by the stove or the hollow place worn in the gravel near the door where his little cat had loved to scratch and roll.

But that's not the end of the story, not quite.

12

Joe rowed home fast, talking all the time to Lily Black, who sat facing him and never took her eyes off his face. When they got ashore she scampered up the path ahead of him to the house with her tail in the air. She knew perfectly well where she was.

Of course, there was a great reunion. Never had Lily had so much loving in her life, or so much food all at once. Her family was so excited they kept interrupting each other and would hardly give Joe a chance to tell about the old man and his boat, and how Lily had stayed with him all winter and how much he loved her, but they finally got the story straight. Meantime Lily was stuffing herself with all kinds of good things that Joe had put down for her, and after that she went padding all around the house looking at everything; they could hear her in the next room, her paws pattering lightly in a single-foot beat. After she had satisfied herself that things were as they should be she spread herself out on Joe's bed, washed her face and paws and went to sleep, as though she hadn't been away at all.

"You see?" said Pa, as he walked by the door and saw her in there. "Just what I always said. We run a first-class hotel for Miss Lily Black, our Upside-Down Cat." But this time he laughed as he said it.

38

Joe, during the next few days, was bothered about something. The old fisherman had taken care of Lily Black all winter — wonderful care — and so perhaps she really belonged to *him*. He had hated to part with her, Joe could tell from the abrupt way he'd done it, and wasn't the old man feeling now the way he himself had felt last fall when Lily disappeared? He brooded about it a lot. He didn't tell anybody, but he made a plan.

This is what he did. He kept track of the days when the *Lettie V.* came into The Basin. Then he began going out himself in the punt on those days, and he and the old man would wave to one another, very formally, from a distance. After a while they brought their boats together and got to talking, mostly about Lily, but about other things too, and they became good friends. Oddly enough, the old man didn't have a single grandson. He had five granddaughters and he doted on them, but in his heart he always wished he had had a grandson, a small boy in the family hanging around. He began to take a shine to Joe, and he was always glad to see the bright-colored punt and its red-haired oarsman coming out to waylay him. Sometimes he gave him a few lobsters to take home, and you can imagine who got her share.

Then one morning Joe took Lily Black out with him, and the old man was as pleased as Punch to see her and invited them both on board, and they sat peacefully together while the *Lettie V.* drifted at a snail's pace up The Basin on the flood tide, with Joe's punt trailing astern and Lily sitting in her regular place on the afterdeck.

From then on, they went out quite often.

For a while Joe was too shy, and also too scared, to speak to his

39

friend about his worry, but at last he did, the week before he was going to leave. Mother was already throwing out sneakers and bathing suits that wouldn't last another summer and everybody was feeling disrupted and cranky.

On this particular day, one of the last ones, Joe and Lily Black were sitting on the deck of the *Lettie V*. They were all a little subdued. You could tell it was the end of summer by the difference in the light along the shore — now it was pale and hazy.

Joe said quickly, before he really knew he was going to speak, although he had rehearsed the words to himself a hundred times, "I don't feel right about taking Lily away from you." There! He had said it.

"Why not?" said the old man, astonished. "She's your cat, ain't she?"

"Well, she's your cat too, sort of," Joe said. "Maybe *you* should keep her, not me. You saved her life — why shouldn't she be yours?" But he felt so miserable he barely finished that last sentence, and his hand went out to Lily Black's head.

"Now you listen to me," the old man said. "She's not my cat at all. No question about it. I may have made her winter a little easier and by good luck you and I met up and so she got home safe and sound. Don't you think another thing about it. You take her back to the city where she'll be safe and comfortable, just the way she used to be, and when you come back next summer you can bring her out to say hello to me."

"All right, if you say so," Joe answered. "But you take her home with you for a visit *now*, before we leave. And every summer you ought to have her for a while. Then she'll belong to both of us."

The old man shook his head, smiling. "Oh, no," he said. "No, I

41

wouldn't want to do that, Joe. I'd like to see her out here with you once in a while, that's all."

They stopped talking then. Lily turned her back on them and watched the gulls that floated around them. Joe stared at the unlighted pipe the old man was holding loosely in his big hand, and the old man looked at Lily and appeared to be about to say something, but he kept still. This was the first time in Joe's life that it had occurred to him that grown-up people — *old* people — can be as miserable as children can be, and this discovery was something he never forgot. He saw, then, that it was time to leave. He pulled the punt up alongside and jumped in and called to Lily Black, who, undecided for a minute, only turned her head to him. To go or to stay, she seemed to be asking. Joe had to reach over, pick her up, and set her down in the small boat; she was stiff in his arms, not resisting, but not happy either. She got up on the stern thwart and sat there with her tail curled around her front feet.

"So long," Joe said to the old man, taking up his oars. "And I sure want to thank you." The old man didn't answer, but he raised his right hand in a little gesture that might have been "Goodbye," or "God-speed." He started his engine and then remarked, kind of absentmindedly, "You could paint that punt before you leave — then she'd be all ready for you next summer. Haul her out tomorrow, so's she'll dry out good first." So it was really goodbye; he didn't want to see them again that year.

He turned away, and the *Lettie V.* moved off, and all the gulls rose, crying and very white in the sunlight, to follow her.

Joe set out for home, slowly, watching over his shoulder as the big boat's wake spread out wider and wider on the calm water. He started to say something to Lily about the old man, but she was looking fixedly ahead at the great granite ledges and the familiar woods, for she was getting hungry. Anyway, he didn't feel like talking, even to her. He just rowed home.